This book belongs to:

....

....

Written by Jackie Andrews
Illustrated by Jo Davies and Helen Prole
Designed by Branka Surla

Copyright © 1998 Ragdoll Productions (UK) Ltd.
Design of the Tots TV puppets and Tots TV house © 1993
Ragdoll Productions (UK) Ltd.
Tots TV is a trademark and is used under licence.
Based on the Carlton Television Series produced by Ragdoll Productions

Published in Great Britain in 1998 by
World International Limited,
Deanway Technology Centre,
Wilmslow Road, Handforth,
Cheshire SK9 3FB.

Printed in Italy
ISBN 0 7498 3898 1

Tilly, Tom and Tiny's Big Treasure Adventure

Adapted from the original script by
Andrew Davenport
Illustrated by Jo Davies and Helen Prole

CONTENTS

Chapter One
Captain Tom

"Tilly! Tiny!" called Captain Tom as he stood at the wheel of the big sailing ship in his splendid blue uniform.

"All hands on deck! All hands on deck, I said!"

There was a clattering and scuffling.

"On arrive, Tom!" called Tilly.

"Coming, Tom, coming!" said Tiny.

Tilly and Tiny raced across the deck, while high up in the rigging, Furryboo secretly slid neatly down one of the ropes so he could see what was going on.

"À vos ordres, Capitaine!" said Tilly, coming smartly to attention.

"Oh, yeah," said Tiny. "Aye, aye, Captain Tom!"

"A-ha-ha, me hearties … " Tom began, but before he could say what he wanted to say, Tiny interrupted him.

"Excuse me, Captain Tom, but why have you got that funny hat on?"

"This is not a funny hat, if you don't mind. This is my Captain's hat and I am very important, I am. I'm the captain of this great big ship … so I say what jobs you have to do … and then you have to do them."

"Oh, yeah. Jobs, jobs, jobs!" said Tiny, excited.

Tilly held up her telescope.

"Moi, je suis Tilly avec mon télescope!" She put it to her eye and looked round at the horizon.

"Tell you what, Tilly," said Tom. "You can have a very, very special job, OK? You can be the Lookout."

"Oh, Tilly la vigie. Oh, oui, oui, oui, oui, oui." Tilly was very pleased to be the Lookout.

Tiny was excited, too. "Oh, Tom, Tom. What important job am I going to do? Look ... I've got my bucket and my brush." He held them up for Tom to see.

"Well, you're a sailor, Tiny, so you have to scrub the decks."

Tiny blinked. "Scrub the decks? *Scrub the decks?*"

"Yes, that's what sailors do, Tiny," Tom explained. "Everyone knows that sailors scrub the decks."

"Oh, all right then," said Tiny doubtfully. "Aye, aye, Captain Tom."

While he and Tilly went off to begin their tasks, Captain Tom sang a little song. Tilly picked up the tune

on her flute and Tiny came and joined Tom in dancing the hornpipe.

"I'm Captain Tom
I'm the captain of the ship
Sailing along on the ocean blue
And I'm the most important
'Cos I've got my special hat on
And I'm busy telling everybody
What to do."

Faster and faster Tilly played, and faster and faster Tom and Tiny danced. Furryboo joined in with a hornpipe of his own, along one of the yardarms, until...

he slipped and fell into Tiny's bucket of soapy water.

SPLOSH!

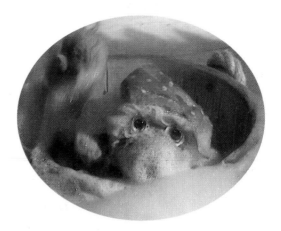

The ship sailed across the calm ocean. As the breeze picked up, Captain Tom knew it was time to set more sail.

"Sailor Tilly, Sailor Tiny! Prepare to let down the sails!"

"À vos ordres, Capitaine!"

"Aye, aye, Captain!"

Tilly and Tiny hauled on the ropes. The big white sails shivered and shook, and then filled with the breeze.

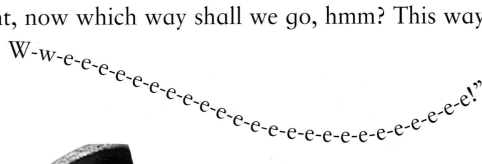

"Regarde!" whispered Tilly.

"Yeah, Tilly, look at all those great big sails," gasped Tiny. "We did that, Tilly."

"Oui!"

Tom practised steering the ship.

"Right, now which way shall we go, hmm? This way, I think.   W-w-e-e-e-e-e-e-e-e-e-e-e-e-e-e-e-e-e-e-e-e-e-e-e-e-e-e-e-e-e!"

He turned the wheel to the left. The big ship leaned heavily to port, and Tilly and Tiny tumbled across the deck.

"O-o-o-o-o-o-oh-h-h-h!" they cried.

Furryboo clung tightly to the rigging.

"No, this way I think," said Tom, and he turned the wheel to the right. The ship listed over to starboard. Tilly and Tiny were flung across to the other side.

"W-o-o-a-a-e-e-e-o-o-o!"

Suddenly, Tilly fell head-first into a barrel.

"Tilly, Tilly!" called Tiny as he saw Tilly's legs waving in the air. "Are you all right?"

"Ooops," muttered Tom, and he held the wheel still. "Oh dear. Sorry, Tilly."

Furious, Tilly slowly emerged from the barrel. "Tom, fais plus attention, s'il te plait ... !"

"Yes, Tom, actually. If you're going to be the captain of a great big ship, you have to be a bit more careful with the steering. You can't be the Captain if you're going to mess about, can you? Otherwise, I'll be Captain." He giggled.

"Oh, absolument non, Tiny!" said Tilly firmly.

"Oh." Tiny's face fell. He really thought he'd make a good captain.

"Excuse me," interrupted Tom. "I'm the captain, you know, and I'm in charge."

"Yes. And don't we know it!" snapped Tiny.

Chapter Two
An Adventure!

On and on they sailed. Tiny stood at the ship's side and watched the waves endlessly rolling away in their wake. The sea went on for ever and ever.

"Excuse me, Captain Tom?" he said.

"Yes, Sailor Tiny?"

"Um, where are we going?"

"Oh Tiny, we're going on a great big adventure!"

"Are we nearly there yet?"

"Tiny, Tiny! The thing about adventures is that you never know when they're going to happen. I mean, it could happen any time," Tom explained.

"Cor!" said Tiny. An adventure could happen any time!

From his secret place in the rigging, Furryboo waved his tail happily. He liked adventures, too.

"Sailor Tilly!" called Captain Tom. "Look across the sea with your telescope, to see what you can see."

"Oui, mon capitaine!" said Tilly smartly. She put her telescope up to her eye and slowly looked all round the horizon.

"Je suis Tilly," she sang, "avec mon télescope. Je regarde! Je regarde!"

"Can you see anything, Tilly?"

"Non, Capitaine!" Tilly replied.

"Oh all right, then. Keep looking."

"À vos ordres!"

While Tilly watched with her telescope at the bow, Tiny leant his bucket on the rail and looked over the side of the ship. Suddenly, some playful dolphins sped past. Tiny and Tilly sang a gently-sailing-across-the-water kind of song together as the great big ship continued on its way.

"La mer, la mer
Everywhere –
Everywhere the sea.
La mer, la mer
Everywhere –
We're sailing on the sea.

The sound of the wind in the sails
Blowing us along
The sea goes on forever
We're sailing on and on and on.

La mer, la mer
Everywhere –
Everywhere the sea."

Suddenly, Tilly spotted something in her telescope.

"Ooh là là ! Ooh! Qu'est-ce que c'est?"

"What, Tilly?" asked Tiny.

"Regarde dans l'eau!"

"Look in the water? Oooh, what's that?"

Tilly joined Tiny at the rail and they both looked down into the water. There was a bottle bobbing about in the waves.

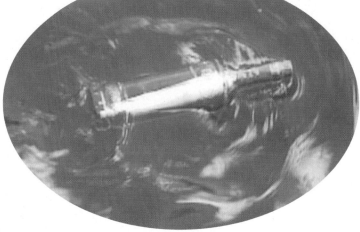

"Qu'est-ce que c'est?"

"I don't know what it is, Tilly," said Tiny, "but it looks like a little bottle in the water."

"Umm, Tiny? Attrape-la dans ton seau." Tilly suggested.

"Oh yes, Tilly, that's a good idea. I could catch it in my bucket. Let's try."

Tiny carefully let down his bucket on a rope and managed to catch the bottle with it. He pulled the bucket back up.

But when he took out the bottle, they could both see that there was a piece of paper inside it. A message!

"Cor, Tilly. A message in a bottle. This could be an adventure coming up!"

"Allez! Viens!"

"Yeah, quick. Captain Tom!"

They ran to find Captain Tom, who was busy steering the ship. Tiny waved the bottle at him and explained what they had found.

"Oh, wow! A message in a bottle?" cried Tom.
"Yeah, Tom. Isn't it exciting?" said Tiny.
"Where did it come from?" asked Tom.
"Well," said Tiny and he sang,

♪ "Tilly was looking and looking and looking
And looking across the sea
She was looking and looking and looking and looking
And then she called to me.
And I was looking and looking and looking and looking
And looking across the sea
I was looking and looking and looking and looking
And guess what I did see.

I saw a little bottle
Bobbing along in the sea
So I caught it in my bucket
To see what it might be ..." ♪

"And then we came to see you, Tom."

Tom shook his head with wonder as he examined the bottle. "Tots," he said, "this is definitely a message in a bottle."

"Oooh – ouvre-la, ouvre-la!"

"Yeah – open it, Tom, open it!"

Tom grasped the cork and pulled and pulled.

"Just opening it, Tots," he said. He pulled and pulled again, heaving and straining. Suddenly,

the cork came out with an enormous

POP!

Tom fell over backwards.

"Are you all right, Tom?" asked Tiny anxiously. "Did you get it open?"

Tom picked himself up and straightened his uniform coat.

"Yes, Tots, I did," he said. "Right, let's see what it says."

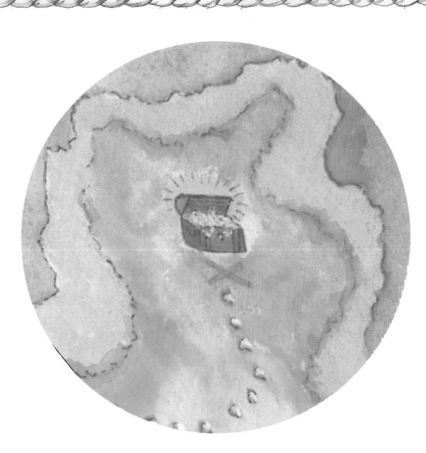

As Tom carefully spread the piece of paper open on a box lid, they gasped.

"C'est une carte!" whispered Tilly.

"Yes, this is a map, Tots. But Tots, this isn't an ordinary map," said Tom, mysteriously. "This is a secret treasure map."

"Cor! A secret treasure map!" said Tiny.

Tom pointed out all the details of the map to them. It was, he explained, a plan of an island. Here was a path marked leading to the treasure, and here was a picture of the treasure itself. A cross marked the spot where the treasure was buried. In the top left corner, in a circle, was a small drawing of the island itself. The Tots looked at the map and thought hard about that chest of gold and jewels.

"Tom, Tilly," said Tiny, "it would be brilliant if we could find some secret treasure – wouldn't it?"

"Yes, Tiny. Yes, that would be a really good adventure. Yeah!" Tom agreed.

"Tilly?" Tiny looked round. Where had Tilly gone?

Tilly was at her lookout post, focusing her telescope.

"Oh là là là là!" She had spotted something very exciting. "Tom, Tiny! Oh là là! Oh non! Oh, oui! Venez! Venez!"

Tom and Tiny raced along the deck to join her.

"What is it, Tilly? What?" called Tiny.

Tilly pointed ahead. "Là!" she cried.

Tom and Tiny stared hard, not quite able to believe what they could see.

"It's that secret island," said Tom. "Look. It's the one on the map."

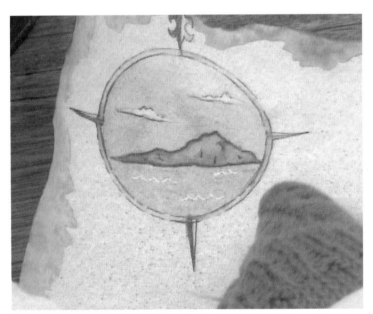

"I don't believe it!" said Tiny. "It's the secret treasure island!"

"Oh là là là là!"

Tom straightened up and adjusted his Captain's hat. "Do you know what, Tots?" he said. "I can feel an adventure coming on!"

"Une aventure!"

"Adventure!"

Chapter Three
Secret Paths

 "Three Tots looking for a chest full of gold
    Yo-ho-ho! Yo-ho-ho!
    Three Tots fearless, brave and bold
    Yo-ho-ho! Yo-ho-ho!"

Sailor Tilly and Sailor Tiny pulled their
rowing boat up on to the sandy beach
and then Captain Tom climbed out.
They had arrived at the secret treasure island!
    "Wait, wait, wait!" said Tom, before the others could
rush off and explore. "It's time for me to do my special
speech."
    "Why?" asked Tiny.

"Pourquoi?" asked Tilly.

"Because I'm the Captain, right? And captains always give special speeches when they land on treasure islands. They do."

"Oh. All right, then."

Tom drew himself up and looked important, as if he was addressing a large crowd.

"Draw near, Tots and listen well
To your captain brave and true
We're here to find the treasure
And that is what we'll do!"

(Tilly and Tiny nodded. "Definitely!"
"Ah, oui!" they said.)

"But Tots, we know that we won't rest
Until we find that secret treasure chest!"

"Hooray!"

"Bravo!"

"That was a really good speech, Tom," said Tiny. "I feel all brave now."

"Do you? Then let's go find the treasure, Tots."

"Oh, oui, d'accord, Tom. Où est la carte?" asked Tilly.

"Oh yes, Tom. Where's the map?"

"What map?"

"What do you mean, what map?" said Tiny. "The treasure map!"

Tom suddenly felt very uncomfortable. He patted his coat pockets and looked around him. "Oh... um... the treasure map. Um."

"Tom, qu'est-ce que tu as fait avec la carte au trésor?" Tilly demanded.

"Yes, Tom, what have you done with the treasure map?"

"Um, Tots, I think it's back on the big boat," said Tom, gazing at the large expanse of sea they had just rowed across.

"Tom. Banane!"

"Yes, Tom, you big banana. We've come all this way, rowing in that boat and everything, and you're supposed to be looking after the treasure map and you've forgotten all about it!"

"Capitaine Saucisson!" said Tilly, scornfully.

"Yes, you big Captain Sausage!"

"Don't you call me Captain Sausage!" said Tom. "I'm very important, I am!"

While they were arguing, they did not see the ship's bucket bobbing along in the surf behind them. Inside was a very special, secret sailor – Furryboo! He had brought the treasure map with him. Once ashore, he quietly pushed the map along the sand until it rested at Tom's feet. Then he scuttled away.

Tom looked down. He blinked. That looked like the treasure map! "Hey, the map! I've found the map!" he cried and picked it up.

"How did it get there?" asked Tiny.
"I don't know, but let's have a look at it, me hearties."

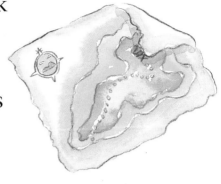

Tilly and Tom watched over Tom's shoulder as he unrolled the map and checked the details again.

The first thing they had to do was to find the secret path. Just the job for Tilly the Lookout!
Tilly swept her telescope over the sand dunes, rocks and trees which lined the beach. Suddenly,

she spotted the row of stones which marked the secret path.

"Regarde! Le chemin secret!" she called.

"That's definitely the secret path," said Tom, comparing it with the map. "All hands, follow the secret path!"

They set off, up the beach and into the dunes, singing their brave song:

"Three Tots looking for a chest full of gold
   Yo-ho-ho! Yo-ho-ho!
   Three Tots fearless, brave and bold
   Yo-ho-ho! Yo-ho-ho!
   Yo-ho-ho! Yo-ho-ho!
   Yo-ho-ho! Yo-ho-HO!"

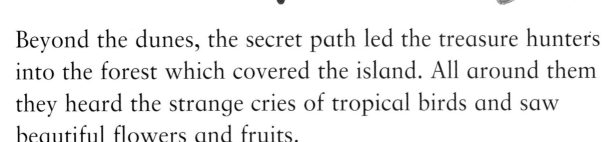

Beyond the dunes, the secret path led the treasure hunters into the forest which covered the island. All around them they heard the strange cries of tropical birds and saw beautiful flowers and fruits.

"Tom, Tiny, cette île au trésor est vraiment belle," said Tilly.

"Yeah, Tilly, this treasure island is really beautiful," Tom agreed.

"Oh it is. It's really lovely," said Tiny. "I just want to stop and look around for a minute. Look at all the lovely island."

"Listen to the birds," said Tom.

"Écoute la mer," said Tilly.

"I think this is the most beautiful place that I've ever been. Ever, ever," said Tiny.

"Oh, Tiny, Tom. C'est le paradis," said Tilly.

"Yeah. Paradise."

The three Tots just couldn't help singing and dancing together – it was such a beautiful island.

Even Furryboo, hidden in the leaves, tapped his paws in time to the music.

 "Here we are
　　On est là
　　Here we are
　　In our island paradise
　　It's absolutely beautiful!
　　It's-a really really nice!
　　On est là
　　Here we are
　　Here we are
　　In our island paradise!"

They were enjoying themselves so much that they forgot
all about maps and treasure and secret paths.

"Le trésor!" cried Tilly, suddenly remembering.

"The treasure!" said Tiny.

"Yeah, we're supposed to be finding the treasure. I completely forgot," said Tom. "Quick! Where's the secret path?"

They looked around them and eventually Tom spotted the line of stones marking their route.

"There it is. We need to go all the way down there to find the secret treasure. Come on, Tots!"

Tilly and Tiny stepped into line behind Captain Tom and they continued their way along the secret path, singing their brave song once more:

"Three Tots looking for a chest full of gold
  Yo-ho-ho! Yo-ho-ho!
  Three Tots fearless, brave and bold
  Yo-ho-ho! Yo-ho-ho!

  Yo-ho-ho! Yo-ho-ho!
  Yo-ho-ho! Yo-ho-HO!"

Chapter Four
Wait for me!

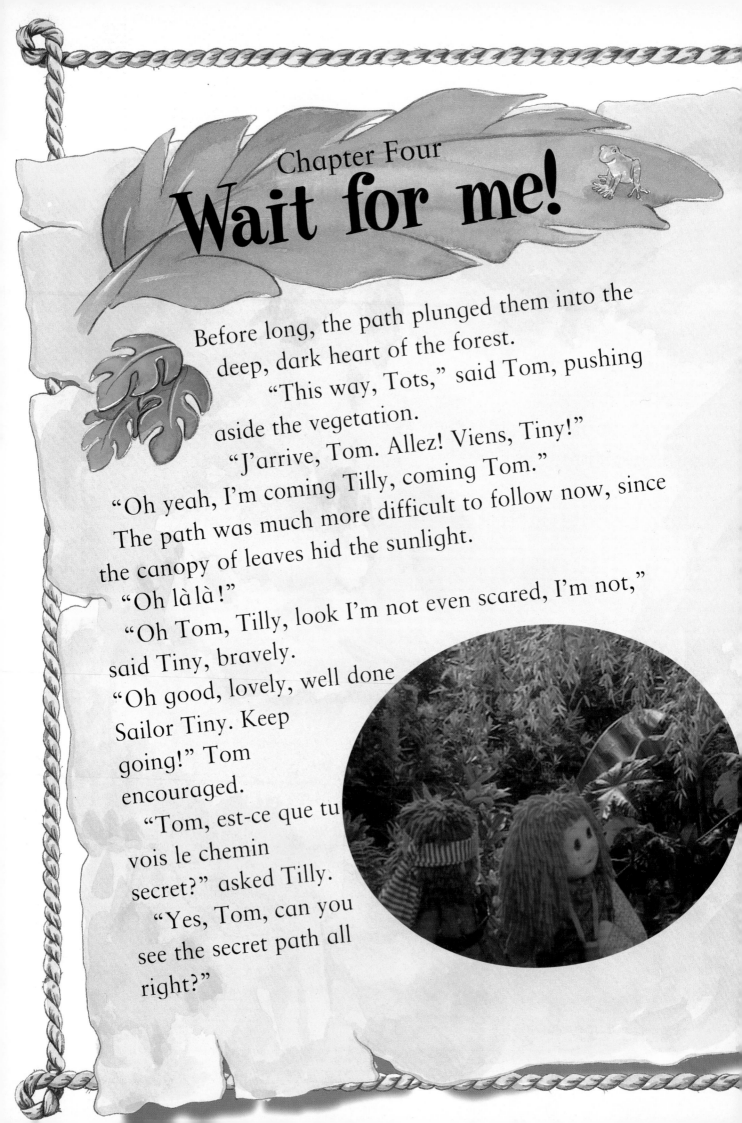

Before long, the path plunged them into the deep, dark heart of the forest.

"This way, Tots," said Tom, pushing aside the vegetation.

"J'arrive, Tom. Allez! Viens, Tiny!"

"Oh yeah, I'm coming Tilly, coming Tom."

The path was much more difficult to follow now, since the canopy of leaves hid the sunlight.

"Oh là là!"

"Oh Tom, Tilly, look I'm not even scared, I'm not," said Tiny, bravely.

"Oh good, lovely, well done Sailor Tiny. Keep going!" Tom encouraged.

"Tom, est-ce que tu vois le chemin secret?" asked Tilly.

"Yes, Tom, can you see the secret path all right?"

"Ah, there – look. It's going off that way," said Tom and he forged ahead.

"Cor, brilliant adventure," said Tiny. "Wait for me!"

The path disappeared into some thick foliage.

"This way!" called Tom from somewhere ahead.

"Dépêche-toi, Tiny!" called Tilly.

"I'm coming, I'm coming!" said Tiny, struggling with the branches and leaves in his way. "Tom, Tilly, wait for me."

Suddenly, Tiny found himself clear. But he could not see Tom or Tilly anywhere.

"Tom? Tilly?" he called, frantically. "Where are you? Oh, no. Oh, no. Where have they gone? Tom? Tilly? I'm feeling a little bit scared now.

Where's the path? Oh, I knew this was going to happen. Tom? Tilly? Don't leave me! Oh no, now I'm all on my own and it's all gone wrong."

Tiny sat down unhappily on a fallen log. But he wasn't quite as alone as he thought. Furryboo had scurried back and was watching from one of the branches nearby, to make sure he was all right.

"Now what am I going to do? I'm completely lost. Maybe I should sing a little song to cheer myself up a bit. Yeah, that's a good idea."

Nervously, Tiny began to sing:

🎵 *"If you're having an adventure*
And everything goes wrong
All you have to do is sing a song.

There's no need to be frightened
Or worried or upset
All you have to do is sing a song.

You might be lost
Or on your own
Or really, really worried
Especially if the place
you're lost
Is dark and damp and
horrid.

So if you're lost on an
adventure
And you feel a little
scared
All you have to do is sing
a song
All you have to do is sing a
song." 🎵

"There. I suppose I feel a little bit better now," he said to himself. He looked around at the trees and plants. "It's very quiet here. Quite nice, really."

Suddenly, a loud animal cry made him jump.

"Oh, what was that? Oh, I do wish Tom and Tilly were here." The nearby bushes rustled and moved.

"Oh no, there's something in there. Oh no! Go away! Don't eat me up! Oh no!" Tiny sprang up and backed away from the bush.

"Tiny! Ooh là là ! Tu es là ?" called Tilly as she pushed her way through the leaves.

"Tiny, there you are!" said Tom, emerging behind her.

"Tom! Tilly!" cried Tiny, and he ran towards them. "Oh, I'm so happy to see you. I was really, really worried."

"Were you?" said Tom. "We were worried about you."

"Not as worried as I was. I had to sing a song."

"Ooh là là ," said Tilly. "On y va?"

"Yeah. Shall we go?" said Tiny.

"All hands stay together!" commanded Captain Tom.

"Definitely aye aye, Captain!"

"À vos ordres, Capitaine!"

Chapter Five
Open the Box!

Furryboo sniffled and snuffled his way along the secret path, following the trail of stones. He came to a large cross marked in sand on the ground. This must be the place where the treasure was buried! Wasting no time, Furryboo began to dig, tossing the dark, leafy soil this way and that.

Faster and faster he dug, down and down into the ground.

Suddenly, the ground gave way underneath him and Furryboo disappeared in a cloud of dust and dirt. He picked himself up, shook the dirt from his coat and

looked around, sniffing. There was definitely something very interesting in this hole. Then he ducked out of sight as he heard the Tots approaching.

"This way," called Tom. "Follow Captain Tom!"

"On arrive, Capitaine, on arrive!"

"Aye aye, Captain Tom!"

Tilly, Tom and Tiny had been walking for ages and ages. Tiny felt it must be time they reached the spot where the treasure was buried. Tom consulted the map again and reckoned that they must indeed be very near.

"I actually think the treasure must be somewhere round here, Tots," he said, studying the map.

"You think the treasure's around here, Tom?" asked Tiny.

"Ooh là là," whispered Tilly.

"Yes, I'm just looking at the map. Hang on a minute. We've come this way w-h-e-e-e w-a-a-a-o-o!"

Tom had stepped back, right into Furryboo's hole, and dropped out of sight.

"Tom?"

"Tom?"

Tilly and Tiny were baffled. Where had Tom gone so suddenly?

"I've fallen down a hole! Tilly? Tiny?" Tom's voice came up to them from deep in the ground. Tilly and Tiny stepped up and looked gingerly over the edge of the hole.

"Tom, what are you doing down there? How did that happen?" asked Tiny.

"I don't know," moaned Tom. "I just sort of fell."

"Oh, Tom. On va t'aider," said Tilly.

"Yes Tom, don't worry – we'll help you. Take Tilly's hand."

Tilly leant over the hole and stretched her hand out as far as she could. Tom reached up on tiptoe, but try as he might he couldn't reach Tilly's hand.

"It's no good. I can't reach. Oh, dear, Tots. I've fallen down a hole and I can't get out," said Tom miserably.

"Don't worry, Tom, I know just what to do," said Tiny.

*"If you're having an adventure
   And you've fallen down a hole
   All you have to do is sing a song.
   There's no need to be frightened
   Or worried or upset
   All you have to do is sing a song!"*

Listening to Tiny singing, and Tilly playing her flute, Tom suddenly realised he was sitting on something. He felt about in the darkness. It was a wooden chest!

"Tots, I think I've found something!"

"Qu'est-ce que c'est?" asked Tilly.

"What is it, Tom?" asked Tiny.

"It's ... it's ... it's the treasure! I've found it!"

"Treasure?" Tilly and Tiny could hardly believe it.

They looked down and saw the wooden chest at the bottom of the hole, and Tom busily brushing off the dirt from its lid.

"We found the treasure! We found the treasure!" sang Tiny. "Brilliant!"

With much heaving and puffing and hauling, they managed to drag the chest and Tom out of the hole.

Furryboo watched them from an overhead branch.

"Well done, Tots," said Tom.

"Ouvre-la, ouvre-la!" said Tilly, bursting with excitement.

"Open the box! Open the box!" said Tiny.

"Right then. Here we go," said Tom and he carefully lifted up the heavy lid.

A golden glow lit up the faces of the Tots as they gazed down at the fine gold and jewels which shone and shimmered at them. Rubies, sapphires, diamonds, emeralds and strings of pearls. Red, green, gold, blue and silver. They were all here.

"Ooooh là là là là là!" said Tilly softly.

"That's the treasure, that is," said Tom.

"Oh, c'est magnifique!"

"That's definitely the treasure," said Tiny.

"Hey, Tots. I think I feel a speech coming on," said Tom.

"Oh, yes, Tom. That is definitely a good idea, because finding treasure is a very special occasion."

"Oui, oui."

Tom drew himself up once more, making himself look important. He cleared his throat:

"We've found the secret treasure
   The purpose of our trip
   And now we have the pleasure
   Of returning to our ship!"

"Hooray!" cried Tilly and Tiny.
"Now pack up the treasure, and let's go!"
"Aye aye, Captain Tom! Ha ha!"

Chapter Six
Splash!

On board the big ship once more, Captain Tom and his crew couldn't help having another peek at the lovely, secret treasure.

"Oooh là là," said Lookout Tilly.

"Que c'est jolie."

"I really like this treasure," said Sailor Tiny. "It's absolutely glittery!"

"Oui, Tom, Tiny. C'était vraiment une excellente aventure."

"Yeah," said Tom. "It was an excellent adventure. We found the secret treasure didn't we, Tots?"

"Yes, we did."

"Tots, now do you know what?" asked Tom.

"What?"

"Quoi?"

"Time to go home now!"

"Hooray!"

"Bravo!"

Tilly and Tiny jumped up and down joyfully.

"All hands on deck!" roared Captain Tom. "Set sail for home!"

"À vos ordres, Capitaine!"

"Aye aye, Captain!"

But instead of rushing off to help Tilly with the sails, Tiny hung back, shuffling his feet and looking awkward.

"Oh Tom, Tom, Tom, Tom," he began, "I've just thought of something I wanted to ask you."

"Oh yes, Sailor Tiny?"

"Um ... I was just wondering. I know that the Captain is a very important job and everything, and I know that normally the Captain does the steering, but I was just wondering if I could do the steering on the way home, because I haven't had a go yet. I'd be careful and concentrate. Please?"

Tom thought about Tiny's request for a bit. "Yes, all right then, Sailor Tiny, as long as you are careful."

"Yes, yes, yes, I will be very, very careful. Oh thank you, thank you, thank you, Tom!"

Tiny gave Tom a big kiss and sped away to take the wheel.

Up in the rigging, Furryboo covered his eyes with his paws. He had a good idea what was coming.

"Lower the sails!" commanded Captain Tom. "Set sail for home!"

"À vos ordres, Capitaine!" cried Tilly.

"Aye aye, Captain Tom!" called Tiny. "Here we go ..."

Tiny threw his weight on to the wheel so that it spun sharply to the right. The big ship tilted over to starboard and Tilly and Tom slid across the deck.

"SAILOR TINY!" roared Captain Tom, holding tightly to his hat.

"Oh, non! ··· A-a-a-a-g-h!"

shrieked Tilly as Tiny swung the wheel the other way and the ship listed over to port.

The secret treasure chest slid across the deck, too.

Across the deck – and out through a porthole, where it fell straight into the sea.

SPLASH!

As it drifted down and down, the lid came open and the gorgeous, glittery jewels sparkled and gleamed.

Furryboo hid his head.

Tom and Tilly ran to the ship's side and looked over, but the chest had completely disappeared.

"Oh dear," said Tiny in a small voice.

"Tiny!" said Tom.

"Qu'est-ce que tu as fait?" said Tilly. "Quelle banane! Oh non!"

"Yes, Tiny, you great big banana! Now look what you've done. Look!"

"Oh dear, I'm ever so sorry. I didn't mean to make the treasure go in the water. Well, steering a big ship is very difficult when you've never done it before."

The three Tots looked mournfully over the ship's side. There didn't seem to be anything they could say to make things better.

"You know what, Tots?" said Tom after a while. "It's only treasure, isn't it? I mean, you know, it's nice to look at ... but it's not much use really, is it?"

Tilly and Tiny blinked in surprise.

"Well, now you mention it, Tom," said Tiny, "I suppose it isn't much use really, is it, treasure ... and we did have a really good adventure, didn't we?"

"Oui! J'ai une idée!" said Tilly, suddenly.

"Ooh, you've got an idea, Tilly?"

"Oui. Tom, où est la carte?"

"Map? Um ... the map ..." Tom patted his coat and pockets, then he pulled out the rolled-up map. "Here it is. The map."

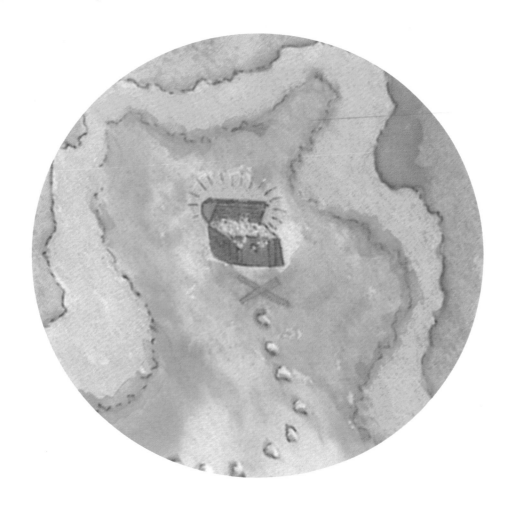

"What do you want the map for, Tilly?"

Tilly took the map and laid it out flat. "Alors. Regardez la carte." She pointed to the cross where the treasure was buried. "Avant, le trésor etait là," she said.

"That's where the treasure used to be," said Tom, as Tilly carefully rubbed out the cross.

"Oui, et maintenant, le trésor est là," said Tilly, marking in a new cross where the treasure fell into the sea.

"Now the treasure is here!" said Tom.

"Yeah! Under the sea!" added Tiny.

Tilly rolled up the map again and put it back in the

bottle. She pushed the cork firmly in the top.

"Prêt, Tom?" she asked. "Prêt, Tiny?"

"Ready, Tilly, ready!" they replied, laughing.

"Allez, une ... deux ... trois ...!" and Tilly threw the bottle with its message back into the sea.

SPLASH!

"Oh Tom, Tilly, now somebody else will be able to find the secret treasure map, won't they? And then they'll be able to have an adventure finding the treasure!"

"Oh oui, Tiny."

"It was a good idea of yours, Tilly," said Tom. "And now, Tots – it's time to set sail!"

"Oh, oui – à vos ordres, Capitaine!" said Tilly, smartly.

"Aye aye, Captain Tom!" said Tiny.

And high above their heads, Furryboo sniffed and waved his tail happily.

"Umm ... Tom, Tiny ..." Tilly began. "Cette fois c'est moi qui navigue."

Tilly's turn to steer? Tom opened his mouth to say something, then shut it again. He blinked and looked at Tiny.

"It's true, Tom," said Tiny. "It's Tilly's turn to steer now."

Tom nodded. "Right then, Tots, let's sail for home!"

"Good idea. Aye aye, Captain Tom."

Tilly, Tom and Tiny's Big Treasure Adventure Game

How to Play

To play this exciting game for two or more players you will need a dice and a different coloured counter for each player.
Place your counters on board ship.
Youngest player starts.
Take turns to throw the dice and move your counters round the board, following any orders on the spaces where you land.
The first player to return to the ship wins the game.

40

39
Toss the bottle with the map back into the sea. Go to 40.

38
You b
banana!
treasure's
overboar
back to

23

22

27

24
You've forgotten the map.
Go back to 19.

25
You find the treasure map at your feet.
Go to 27.

26
You spy the secret path.
Go to 29.

2
Stop t
at the f
Miss

21
Sing, "Yo-ho-HO!" and row to 23.

20

19

18
You spy the secret island with your telescope. Sail on to 22.

17